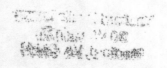

A Beginning-to-Read Book

Come to School, Dear Dragon

by Margaret Hillert

Illustrated by David Helton

NORWOOD HOUSE PRESS

DEAR CAREGIVER, The *Beginning-to-Read* series is a carefully written collection of classic readers you may remember from your own childhood. Each book features text comprised of common sight words to provide your child ample practice reading the words that appear most frequently in written text. The many additional details in the pictures enhance the story and offer the opportunity for you to help your child expand oral language and develop comprehension.

Begin by reading the story to your child, followed by letting him or her read familiar words and soon your child will be able to read the story independently. At each step of the way, be sure to praise your reader's efforts to build his or her confidence as an independent reader. Discuss the pictures and encourage your child to make connections between the story and his or her own life. At the end of the story, you will find reading activities and a word list that will help your child practice and strengthen beginning reading skills.

Above all, the most important part of the reading experience is to have fun and enjoy it!

Shannon Cannon

Shannon Cannon,
Literacy Consultant

MAR 2 8 2007

Norwood House Press • P.O. Box 316598 • Chicago, Illinois 60631
For more information about Norwood House Press please visit our website at
www.norwoodhousepress.com or call 866-565-2900.

LIBRARY OF CONGRESS CATALOGING-IN-PUBLICATION DATA

Hillert, Margaret.
  Come to school, dear dragon / by Margaret Hillert ; illustrated by David
Helton.—Rev. and expanded library ed.
     p. cm.—(Beginning to read series. Dear dragon)
  Summary: A boy's pet dragon visits him at school and joins in the
classroom activities. Includes reading exercises.
  ISBN-13: 978-1-59953-017-8 (library edition : alk. paper)
  ISBN-10: 1-59953-017-1 (library edition : alk. paper)
  1. Readers (Primary) [1. Readers.] I. Helton, David, ill. II. Title. III. Series.
PE1119.H57855 2006
  [E]—dc22
                            2005033587

Oh, Father.
This is good.

Now I have to go.
I want this—
        and this—
                and this.

5

I have to go now.
I have work to do.
Away I go.
Away, away, away.

Come on.
You can come with me.
Run, run, run.

This is the spot.
I will go in here.
You can not come in,
but do not go away.
I will come out.

I like it here.
I see my friends.
We have work to do,
but we have fun, too.

We work and we play
and we have fun here.

Oh, what is this?
Why are you here?
Why did you come in?

You will have to sit down.
Sit, sit.
That is good.

I guess you can help us.
Yes, yes.
You can help.

We will make something.
It will look like you.
Yes, you are
a help to us.

Here is a book.
Books are fun to read.
We like to read books.

And look at this.
Look in here.
This one looks something like you.

Now we will go out.
We will go out to play.
Come on out with me.

You can help us.
Here is something you can do.
You are a big help.

Here are three balls.
One, two, three balls.
Red, yellow, and blue.
We will play with
the balls.

Do this for us.
Help us with this.
We want to play this way.

23

Now we will go.
We can walk with friends.
It is good to have friends.

We have to stop here.
Stop and look.
Look out for cars.

Here we go.
This way. This way.
On the way to Father.
Father will have something
good for us to eat.

Here you are with me.
And here I am with you.
Oh, what a good day, dear dragon.

READING REINFORCEMENT

The following activities support the findings of the National Reading Panel that determined the most effective components for reading instruction are: Phonemic Awareness, Phonics, Vocabulary, Fluency, and Text Comprehension.

Phonemic Awareness: The /dr/ sound

Substitution: Say the following words to your child and ask him or her to substitute the first sound in the word with /**dr**/:

rip = drip	sift = drift	mop = drop
sag = drag	mess = dress	sank = drank

Phonics: The letter Dd

1. Demonstrate how to form the letters **D** and **d** for your child.

2. Have your child practice writing **D** and **d** at least three times each.

3. Ask your child to point to the words in the book that begin with the letter **d**.

4. Write down the following words and ask your child to circle the letter **d** in each word:

dog	dig	hard	day	ride	did	read
cloud	duck	bird	dime	bed	kid	dear
red	do	down	card	dear	dragon	word

Vocabulary: Story Concepts

1. Ask your child to say words that describe things we do at school. Write the words on separate pieces of paper.

2. Randomly say the words and ask your child to point to the correct word.

3. Ask your child to describe a time when he or she did some of the things that the words describe.

> Possible words:
>
> | | | | |
> |---|---|---|---|
> | read | write | play | math |
> | help | learn | draw | cooperate |

Fluency: Shared Reading

1. Reread the story to your child at least two more times while your child tracks the print by running a finger under the words as they are read. Ask your child to read the words he or she knows with you.

2. Reread the story taking turns, alternating readers between sentences or pages.

Text Comprehension

1. Ask your child to retell the sequence of events in the story.

2. To check comprehension, ask your child the following questions:

   • What did the kids do when Dear Dragon came to the classroom?

   • How did Dear Dragon help the children in the classroom? How can you help in your classroom?

   • What do you like most about school? Why?

WORD LIST

Come to School, Dear Dragon uses the 75 words listed below.

This list can be used to practice reading the words that appear in the text. You may wish to write the words on index cards and use them to help your child build automatic word recognition. Regular practice with these words will enhance your child's fluency in reading connected text.

a	day	I	play	us
am	dear	in	read	walk
and	did	is	red	want
are	do	it	run	way
at	down			we
away	dragon	look	see	what
		like	sit	why
balls	eat		something	will
big		make	spot	with
blue	Father	me	stop	work
book	for	my		
but	friends		that	yellow
	fun	not	the	yes
can		now	this	you
cars	go		three	
come	good	oh	to	
	guess	on	too	
		one	two	
	have	out		
	help			
	here			

ABOUT THE AUTHOR Margaret Hillert has written over 80 books for children who are just learning to read. Her books have been translated into many different languages and over a million children throughout the world have read her books. She first started writing poetry as a child and has continued to write for children and adults throughout her life. A first grade teacher for 34 years, Margaret is now retired from teaching and lives in Michigan where she likes to write, take walks in the morning, and care for her three cats.

Photograph by Glenna Washburn

ABOUT THE ADVISER Shannon Cannon contributed the activities pages that appear in this book. Shannon serves as a literacy consultant and provides staff development to help improve reading instruction. She is a frequent presenter at educational conferences and workshops. Prior to this she worked as an elementary school teacher and as president of a curriculum publishing company.